"Imagination is more important than Knowledge. For knowledge is limited to all we know and understand, while imagination embraces the entire world, and all there will be to know and understand."

- Albert Einstein

LEGENDS

By John Myers

Prologue
-One More Day-

The morning was nice and cold, of course not too cold for my home region. I lived in the far eastern side of The Duganian Empire on my father's plantation. To the north and east of us were The Rift Mountain range, to the south was beaches and forests, we were snuggled in the perfect spot. My father stopped my daydreaming and called up to me that morning; from below my window. I opened up the shutters and let in the rising sun. My father was standing out in the yard getting a horse ready for work in the fields.

"Sera come down here and get to the "twigs*". They need help packing up the harvest for transport!" He yelled up to me while I was staring out my window at the distant mountains that separated Dugania and The Union. It was only me and my dad ever since my mother died so I helped him as much as I could. The elves helped out a lot but mostly on the fields and with the animals.

    I had quickly gotten dressed, ran down the steps and left off towards the main fields. The sun had risen higher and the day became warmer. The sun's rays came through the trees creating a beautiful sight as I walked into the sugar cane fields. The fields were closer to the city close enough to see just the tops of the buildings and the smoke from the chimneys.

    The elves have been working a lot recently due to the upcoming snow storm coming over the mountains. And the weather wasn't the only problem; the world called it Erster Krieg it was a global war spanning from Barbaria in the far north all the way to The Union in the east. Everyone had a lot on their minds.

    I eventually made my way to the outer fields where the workers, who were mostly elves, had begun putting the produce in the wagon. The field storage barn was full of various fruits and vegetables. All the juices had seeped into the wood leaving a vintage sweet smell in the air.

The local Elven Chief of the Shān Tribe approached me in the barn and beckoned me to follow her. "Good morning, young one, I assume you are here to ship the produce into the city?" The chief and I walked out of the barn and the fields were full of elven men picking the fruit and placing them in baskets while the women carried them to the wagon. The wagon was almost full and the elves were beginning to get weak. One collapsed and I rushed over to help him up. He was middle aged and very weak; the other elves gave me shady and untrustworthy looks. Most elves did not care for any humans that lived this close to mountains. Later I found his name was Tsuki and had been chased out of his homeland in The Union north after the Dāku Taiyō Massacre. All the elves had to flee The Union or face mass execution under that tyrant King Fredrick. Even after he was assassinated the elves were too scared to return.

It made me so sad to see a once peaceful and proud people forcefully removed from their homes and left to be farm workers and private servants. The produce was packed and placed on the wagon, the chief and Tsuki waved goodbye as I rode off towards the smokestacks of Carvioy.

The city was hundreds of years old and even has its own legends, but that is another story to tell, you could see its age in its people and buildings. The streets were filled with people from all over the empire, every building had its own story and you could feel truly feel it. People were smiling and eating outside restaurants the architecture was a mix of designs from around the world. One building could look Duganian but the one next to it may have a more Mittelland look.

It was wonderful.

My friend met me at the city square; he sat in the shadow of an iron statue of a Duganian soldier holding a Duganian battle flag. He noticed me and waved me down; he got up and ran over to the wagon hopping up in the bag. He spoke the entire way to the trade post my father owned.

"Why doesn't your father get one of those automobiles to transport food?" He asked while he stuffed his face with fruit from one of the baskets. I slapped the fruit out of his hand and focused on steering the horse. But it was a good question. My father was old fashioned and hated the modern world he always said that *"he would die before joining the world of machines"*.

    Me and my friend rode through the street making our way through the crowd of people. We eventually arrived at the trading post and just in time, the more fresh produce was just about to be sold off. Our trading post was near the city center, just off the side just down a small ally way. We stopped the wagon just outside the alley and my friend went down to tell the other workers we were there. I stayed behind.

    The city became very quiet, it was unnerving, and then I saw why everyone stopped. Medics were coming from the front that was just over the mountains. They came through the center of the city in large automobiles; they were white with *Medic* written on the side. I could see inside one of them I don't even want to talk about what I saw. My friend came out and told me to not look that it could send me into a type of shock. I got off the wagon and went to the back alley to help with restocking.

    Our trading post was the largest in the city so we got the most business out of the posts in the region. We also kept the prices low, even though the people wouldn't say it. The city was starving.

The multiple people working the stand worked hard and well. We had people from ever structure of society, the soldiers, the rich, the poor, and even some Stadtmenschen*. They all needed food and we gave them as much as we could give. Midday rolled around and it became a slow humid afternoon.

I had always gone to a local restaurant every day for lunch. I got the same thing every day, a shish taouk, rift chicken marinated in lemon juice and grilled to perfection; in my opinion it's the best type of kabab. I ate it outside the restaurant on the rim of a fountain. My friend would sit next to me and talk to me about what he did or was going to do that day. He told me he was going to sign up for the Duganian Army and that I should stay in the city for the next few days. He seemed scared I guess I should have known why. With the war growing closer and closer people in the city began to get restless.

I told him that I was not going to leave my dad out there to deal with the farm on his own. He brought up the Union propaganda posters showing up around town, how they were signs that the lines were going to break and that the Union was going to overrun the outskirts of the city. I got pissed, stood up and began yelling at him. I don't even remember why or what I said.

He got up and left I didn't know what happened to him for a long time; he had not returned after that. I finished my meal and went back to work putting a smile on my face and ignoring what had happened. The day continued like nothing was wrong I just did what I did every couple days. Hand out food to those who need it. One old lady came up to me, she was small and frail looking. She asked me what was wrong, that she could see distress in my eyes.

I was suddenly telling her everything that happened, as if I needed to.

The lady came behind the counter and sat down with me. As I told her of my farm and the amount of work I do she nodded and asked "yes but what is wrong?" I took a deep breath.

"I'm scared. Of the war. Of the Union. All of it."

She smiled and rested her hand on mine. "I have been through so many conflicts that this one no longer fazes me." She said with a smirk. "You want to know my secret?" she asked. I nodded.

"Let your fear go and trust in the world." I smiled and looked up. She was gone as if she wasn't there at all.

The day moved on slow at first, every hour became slow.

Dragging on hour after hour.

Eventually the trade post closed and the workers packed up the remaining produce as I headed home. The sun was setting behind me as a rode home with the coins earned today. The sky ahead was dark and tempestuous. Arriving at home I looked once more at the powerful storm over the mountains. Flashes of light came from the horizon. The war was in the mountains. Inside my dad sat looking out the window, listening to the thunderous sounds.

He turned to me and told me…

"One More Day."

PART ONE
REVELATION

CHAPTER ONE

-SERA-

I remember the day my life changed and I never knew it until now. It was the twenty third of November the year of our Lords One thousand Nine hundred Nineteen, very early in the morning. The sun had not even risen above the horizon when my father woke me up in a near frantic state. "Wake up Sera, wake up!" he shouted in a frantic and shaky voice. "We must get to the cellar before the battle heads our way!" I remember running down the stairs while the sound of artillery fired off in the distance, even some shells landed nearby causing the house to shake and some dust to fall from the wooden ceiling.

"Hurry sweetie, I'll be down-". Before my

father could finish his sentence a rouge bullet came through the doorway and struck him in the side of the head.

His lifeless body lay on the floor of the house; his blood ran along the cracks in the wood mixing with my tears as I sat next to him hoping he came back to life. Time seemed to have slowed down as what were only a few minutes felt like a lifetime of agony and suffering. It all sped back up as another bullet came through the window and shattered a glass sitting on an end table in the living room. Soon I could hear the sound of a thousand guns firing as the fighting suddenly engulfed the house. In a panic, I ran down the stairs as my father told me, and I waited for the battle to pass.

Sitting in the groggy and dark cellar, I cried as the battle headed toward my home. My tears stopped due to my fear when artillery shells landed nearby, shaking the dust from the cellar ceiling.

"Retreat!" cried a man outside as the sound of marching became louder and louder.

Looking through a small rusted window, I

could see hundreds of boots run past. The plantation was destroyed and all the elves had fled. Then I saw one man was riding a white horse; *he* was the one yelling retreat. Suddenly the sound of a rifle's explosive blast rippled through the valley and the man fell to the ground in a puddle of blood. He looked me in the eyes, as he died the sadness shook my very soul.

    I clung to the stone cellar wall as artillery fell all around the area; one even broke through my house causing the bricks to cave in. I held on the stone as the ground shook beneath my feet. Eventually the cellar collapsed and I was knocked out cold. While unconscious, I witnessed my father looking down at me from the clouds telling me to awake and face my destiny head on. The clouds that I once saw my father within now turned into a storm, lightning struck all around. I could see flashes of war, the sounds of planes flying at high speeds echoed, and a large white light lit up the area. I saw a city with tall buildings bustling full of people and then with a swish of air they all turned to dust, vaporized by the heat… it was a bomb; a bomb so strong it killed everything within its blast.

~ 15 ~

Then I woke up, a group of men pulled me out of the wreckage, my ears were ringing so I could not make out much of what they were saying, something about an occupation. My eyesight was fuzzy for a little while after all I could see were the colors of their uniforms, black and red. I had never seen any black and red uniforms in any books but the men wearing them were helping so I was not too suspicious. They sat me near a fire and gave me a blanket for warmth and soup to make me feel better, after a few minutes it started to snow.

    The look of the soft white snow falling on the burnt and destroyed area was poetic at best. How the snow clung to the walls of my collapsed home just as it did when it was still standing. As I sat there drinking my soup I noticed the soft crunching of snow behind me. Quickly the soldiers stood, startling me in that instant. They saluted at whoever walked up behind us; since my eyesight started to clear minutes ago, I turned to look at the man they saluted. A tall slightly chubby guy, he wore very fine clothes and a top hat, his nose and cheeks were red from the cold and he looked around thirty years of age.

"Good morn' men, how goes the day." The men were hesitant to respond.

"What's wrong, got frostbite on your tongue?" one answered this time although he stuttered through his reply.

"The morning is good sir, we found this, young lass in the rubble sir…"

The soldiers called him sir, I guessed at the time that he was an important person so I stood up as well, that is when he looked at me. The look in his eyes was very similar to the man on horseback that died outside my window.

"What happened to you, young lady?" he came over and sat down near me. I told him what happened and he nodded as he listened as I started telling about my father, the tears started returning.

"There, there, it's okay to cry" he rested his hand on my back and explained that his own father died not too long ago, that is how this conflict started.

I was shocked by his words. The death of his father caused the invasion. Then it struck me. I was speaking to the king of The Union of Democratic Republics, but I could not understand how such a nice man like him could be the son of the tyrant that his father was. His voice was soothing but in a way strong and inspiring, and his scruffy beard was flecked with snow. As the sun rose to about mid-day the snow had built up quite a bit and the soldiers built a small camp and started to converse with the King, probably about how the newly annexed land would need to be governed. After about ten minutes of conversation a black carriage arrived.

"Ah, he is here, young girl I would like you to meet my younger brother, Kurtis Theodore Black, the prince and top strategist of the Union of Democratic Republics."

In the carriage sat a young boy about my age, an islander which was strange, the driver came around the side, opened the door and lowered the steps. The prince walked down the steps and straightened out his military style clothing; I could clearly see the difference in personality between the two brothers. Kurtis trudged through the deep snow over to the camp where his brother quickly ran up and gave his little brother a great hug, only to be met with a heavy punch to the gut.

"Oh!" The king hunched over from the blow "It is very nice to see you again little brother"

The prince smiled "It's nice to see you as well Winston." This seemed like a regular exchange between the two brothers, they laughed it off and they walked over to a table with a large map placed on top.

"So, little brother, this is Dugania the new lands in the U.D.R., it has ports here and here, and major trade goes through here the nearby city of Car-i-vor-e, I think that is how it's pronounced"

"Carvioy" I said trying to be as respectful as possible.

"Oh, and who is this, Winston?" the prince walked over to where I was sitting near the fire just outside the camp; he bowed to me, a gesture of kindness in The Union of Democratic Republics.

"It is a pleasure to meet you, miss…?" I blushed a bit and tried not to look at his eyes, but I could not resist.

"Æthelweard, Sera Æthelweard." His eyes were so blue; as blue as where the sky meets the ocean, they were so hypnotizing.

"Æthelweard?" he said, "That is old western is it not? I have not heard that language since my great grandfather Ignatius was still alive."

Winston started laughing and leaned into the conversation. "So…are we going to get back to the newly annexed land or are you two going to keep flirting with one another."

Kurt looked annoyed and he turned to his brother. "You never know when to shut up Winston, do you know that." Kurt bowed to me and moved on with his brother's plan.

"So" his brother said, "we have a small problem with the natives in the north and the Duganians here and here, that's why I called you." Kurt carefully observed the map of my land and stated that the native elves in the north will not be a problem to them, but the Duganians will cause problems quickly and without judgment. Winston understood what Kurt meant and called for a few men to join him at the city in a few minutes. The way Kurt ordered the king around it was as if he was the true king and Winston a puppet.

    Kurt rolled up the map on the table and placed it in the back of his carriage. He then pointed at the rows of dead bodies and started talking to the nearby soldiers, but I could not make out what he saying. Two soldiers then walked up to one and lifted the blanket; Kurt soon following behind. He bowed his head to say a prayer the soldiers did as well. When they were done, the body was covered back up and Kurt wiped a tear from his eye.

CHAPTER TWO

-HOME-

He walked back over to me and asked me to follow him to the city, his brother, the king, was to give a speech and announce the annexation of Duganian lands between the other U.D.R. members. Although I did not want to leave my father's home I decided to join him to keep my mind off my father's death.

In the city, the snow fell over dead bodies in the streets, soldiers lined anyone who defied them against the wall and held them at gunpoint. I could not look as I heard the line of rifles fire and the sound of the people falling to the ground, their nails scraping on the bricks of the buildings as they tried to keep themselves up and alive, but ultimately were shot in the head if they still breath.

Kurt flinched at the sound of the rifles, holding his hand in a fist; I could see the tears running down his face, trying to look stoic and calm. I could see the anger in his face as he walked through town. The streets were littered with craters and the once beautiful buildings were now just piles of rubble.

People were being herded through the city like cattle, all moving to the center of town.

"Where is the King my lord?" I asked trying not to look at the surrounding area and people.

"He should be just up ahead, look at this place," a loud scream echoed just before a gunshot silenced it.

"What a shame that this is what became of this once proud and prosperous people, all because their "congress" wanted to kick start a war to put them back on the map, now they have been nearly erased from it."

Kurt's words were true this was all because our government wanted to be noticed and to be recognized as strong… our people killed his father, his sister, and his younger brother. Then we started a war we knew we could not win. As I walk through these dead and decaying streets I only blame ourselves for the sadness brought down on our homes.

"Hello little brother, come to see the big speech I see." Winston and a few other soldiers were setting up a podium and a stage for a speech from himself.

"I could not care for your speech; I am only here for your safety." Kurt was scanning the surrounding buildings for shooters or any potential hiding spots. "Who is he?" there was a small man standing in the darkness looking at the gathering of troops. His face had an angered expression on it and his eyes were like daggers.

Kurt walked up to the old man several guards at his back, "This is currently a restricted zone, and you must leave or be shot." Kurt grabbed the man's arm when he refused to leave. "Fine then I'll escort you out." The man tried to fight back but Kurt was too strong for the older man.

"So, Sera…" Kurt's brother, the king, had

finished working and was now sitting on the edge of the stage. "You like him, don't you?" The king whispered this to me causing me to blush.

"I don't know what you're talking about my lord…" the shakiness of my voice gave me away, I was sure of it.

He was smiling and elbowing my shoulder while saying "come on you do don't you" Winston was as persistent as a small child he didn't stop until Kurt walked over brushing dirt off his coat. He waved down two guards and pointed to a window to the east of the stage.

The guards quickly rushed past Kurt as he ran towards us, "GET DOWN!" he shouted, running as fast as he could. Two loud concussive blasts echoed from the nearby building and the King fell back, blood shooting from his abdomen. On the roof near us, a Duganian sniper sat in wait; he must have waited for hours until the King stepped out into the open. When he did he fired nailing the King in the directly in the chest.

Medics were on the scene in seconds, guards surrounded the King, Kurt, and I to protect us.

Kurt was holding down on the wound trying to stop the bleeding. In that moment, everything seemed to slow down, and my life was changed forever. From what Kurt tells me I fainted, but what I saw was nothing of the sort. Everything around me faded into a white haze, every building and structure was gone and I was standing alone in this white mist. A voice called out to me from the blinding mists, it was calming and familiar but I was sure I had never heard it before.

This disembodied voice told me terrible things about the world, things that happened, and things that have yet to. It sounded scared and worried for the future of mankind, the last few words it spoke to me were this, "The world will end when man gets power only gods should have, this has happened before and it will happen again."

When I awoke, I was in an automobile, the road was smooth and made of cut stone, so I knew that I was in a U.D.R. City. Along the street, tall brickwork buildings stood with signs advertising different businesses. People crammed close to each other to look at the new objects in a shop's window, and thousands walked through the city in synchronization to get to work. It was like an ant colony all working together.

In the center of the city was a large walled off area known as "The Top" to the locals. Its walls were made of thick stone and carved into them were the symbols of the U.D.R. The two towers stood about six stories tall and on their top had large U.D.R. Flags flying, four red stars surrounding a blue circle on a white flag. The red stars symbolize the four countries that came together to create The U.D.R., that's also how it acquired its name, the blue circle in the center symbolizes the unification of the lands, and the white stands for peace on the world. Pretty ironic seeing that they just forcefully annexed their neighbor. Stepping out of the automobile I saw Winston being carried on a stretcher into the west wing of the building.

Starting to walk towards them a guard stopped me. "Listen miss, I don't care that the king and prince like you or invited you here, you are not going in that building"

"Look I know it's your job and all, not letting

me go places but I really need to go with them." The guard stood there with this emotionless face

"Give me one good reason on why you *need* to go with them." The guard asked.

"Because she's with us and I don't think neither the King nor the Prince would like to hear that you stopped our guest from entering this building." I was so focused on the guard l did not notice the second automobile.

Oliver Skinner the King of the Sui'nian Federation had arrived for territorial rights to parts of Dugania and now stood beside me, one hand on my shoulder. He was around my height, with disheveled red hair. He had this smirk on his face that showed that he was in charge at the moment and that nothing could deny his momentary power.

The guard then denied his power telling him "All guests then must wait in the main hall of the main building; any guests that leave the hall will be considered trespassing."

So in other words, if he finds any one on the property without permission to leave the main hall they will be shot on site. The guards escorted us up to the main hall, along the steps were paintings depicting a legend of a once great hero that journeyed to the dark lands bringing back, stories and riches.

The paintings ended with the hero raising an army and overthrowing the current tyrannical king and claiming the throne. "Old tales, none of it happened, or at least that is what the old king said." The Sui'nian king stood looking at the final painting above the doors to the main hall, "now this…" he said "this really did happen…"

The large painting depicted *The Great End*. Two gods, the God of Virtue and the God of Sin fought over control of the Earth. The final battle took place upon a snowy mountainside, the greatest mountain. The battle took days, each hit caused earthquakes around the world, and each blow shattered the havens. Hell rose from the ground ripping apart the land and killing the unworthy. The Two have been said to have killed each other on that mountain and from that day on the world had no order or control.

The guard nudged us in telling us to wait for the king and prince. We waited for hours, just talking and looking at the impressive architecture of the manor. The main hall was decorated with beautiful purple drapery and matching carpet. Wonderful paintings lined the walls of places I have never seen before, the shields in-between each painting caught my eye. The shields were old, very old; some had even started to rust. Looking down the line of shields one in the middle was extremely peculiar; it had the original Duganian crest on it! A small plaque was placed on the back of the shield.

It read *"This shield will be the symbol to the people of the Union of Democratic Republics that the Empire of Dugania will always and forever be an ally in war and politics on the global stage, may the light always guide you to heaven."* I started crying, I blamed my people, I was angry with them, furious at them. The Duganian government said that the U.D.R. started this war but we did, we backstabbed them!

In the midst of my tears I felt a hand hold my shoulder, looking up I saw Kurt also in tears. He sat beside me for a bit, we connected and calm each other down I guess.

He stood up and in a shaken and broken voice told the Sui'nian king and me "My brother Winston has been paralyzed from the waist down, as of now I am the King of the U.D.R., shall we head into the dining hall now." He seemed confident but I could tell something else was wrong. He waved us to follow him through a large doorway with two open doors. Inside was an oblong table stretching down the middle of the room.

"We will have to use this room due to the actual meeting room is still being fixed after that attack." He sat the King down and gestured for me to sit next to him. Not too long later more world leaders arrived at the palace to meet with the King and discuss the Duganian annexation; they were not expecting Kurt to be in power. This discussion was harder than they were hoping. They were all very panicked, for Kurt was a very determined person. At four fifteen in the afternoon the talks began. It was soon clear that each country had its own agendas. Several hours of bickering and yelling eventually led to an agreement.

Mid way through the signing of the treaty a report came in that a Duganian revolution was underway in the city of Carvioy. Kurt dispatched a small army of a mere thousand men to put down the revolution from gaining any speed. - the meeting was put on hold for the day and guards escorted the other leaders to the guest wing in the northern side of the palace. Kurt remained at the table, rubbing his eyes in frustration and exhaustion. I asked him if he was fine and he responded that he would be ok and would just need a bit of rest. It was this moment he showed trust in me and told me what was really happening with Winston.

"He was in a state of shock from the bullet wound and fell into a temporary coma, when he wakes up he will never be able to walk for the rest of his life, and if he doesn't die in the coma he will surly die within the next few years." Kurt was in complete shambles, tears were streaming down his face and he could barely even breathe, which is completely normal for someone who lost everything. I sat down beside him, reassuring him, and I remember what we felt at that moment was love; we did not mention it or recognize it but we both felt it. We both went up to our separate rooms.

The night was long and my mind was clouded with nightmares about fear and terror. Great pain and suffering was to come, genocide of extreme proportions that now one could have foreseen. I woke up in a cold sweat a little after midnight based on the moonlight in my room; my breaths were deep and slow; my hands were shaking violently and the world around me felt more sensitive. Apparently I screamed before waking because a guard came through the doorway with a pistol but upon seeing that no one was there holstered his weapon.

"Are you ok my lord?" In confusion I asked why he called me lord instead of miss like the day before, "Well the King gave you full reign of the palace ground and being of no family connections authorized you a lordship, you technically are part of the high council in The U.D.R." I never would have thought that I would ever be a lord in any country, I was so happy i sent the guard back to work and fell back asleep with no nightmares at all.

The next morning, I was surprised with some new clothes, a white shirt with a black coat and a short black skirt was the choice for today but all the other clothes were fancy and made of fine silk. Walking down the hallway was also a delight as the guards had to salute me as I walked by, Kurt was also beaming with enjoyment as he stood next to Winston in a wheelchair who was also grinning cheek to cheek.

"Look at you!" Winston wheeled closer to me and extended a hand in which I shook "You look like a proper politician, and nice choice with the colonial look…" Kurt grabbed Winston's chair and handed him off to the guard nearby. We then walked to the meeting room where Kurt sat me down at my official seat with a small nameplate that read **Sera Æthelweard Advisor to the King**. Soon after the rest of the world leaders arrived and the talks continued add a few more points to the treaty. A few days later the Duganian Peace Treaty was signed and all the leaders went their separate ways, and in between that Kurt and I got to know each other a little bit better. And yet no one could know what would happen in the years to come.

CHAPTER THREE

-HELL RISING-

Just after my introduction into the Union court, Kurt and I decided to get married; life was wonderful and peaceful. Dugania was rebuilt and sent an ambassador in place of me; we all thought nothing could go wrong; I was even pregnant with two boys although I did not know at the time. Yes, it was the perfect life; well it was until Winston died. The day we learned of my pregnancy Kurt received the news that Winston had fallen ill.

His leg had been cut, and due to his paralysis he could not feel it, and had gotten infected. This infection was spreading too fast for any doctor or medicine and eventually reached his heart. After days of struggling and screaming Winston had died very peacefully and silently. The entire country mourned for him, but Kurt mourned more than anyone in the world. He never left our room.

Days turned into weeks and weeks turned into months, the only time Kurt left the room was to see the birth of our two lovely boys. He named them Leo and Shade, this at least brought his spirits up just a bit. Soon Kurt was back to his usual self. The world still felt vulnerable, we all could feel the ground shifting as armies moved into positions, and the world was preparing for war. They all started to play the propaganda games, sending people to cities and posting posters to get support for their cause. Fearing that his own people would turn against him, he garrisoned troops in the major cities to deter any ability to act.

On December third, just a few years later, he called an emergency meeting for all eastern leaders to try to stop the war from happening. Several days later only three leaders arrived at the summit, King Oliver Skinner was one of them. We hadn't seen each other in over a year, we said our hellos and followed Kurt and the other leaders into the war room.

We all sat down, but Kurt remained standing; with one look at his face I knew something was terribly wrong. Out of the eight countries only four showed up.

Kurt walked around to the Duganian Prime Minister "Weird that you would show up here after the war not just two years ago." The Prime Minister was starting to sweat and panic, Oliver joined in.

"Yeah that is a very good point, why are you here instead of sucking up to your Nepponian buddies up north?" The Prime Minister started to panic and tap his fingers; he stood up and ran to the door but was stopped by guards. The room went silent, every man ready to draw their weapons.

"Come quietly and no one will get hurt here…" a guard approached hand extended with the intent to grab the man's arm. The ambassador, in a panic reached for a button on the side of his leg. The guard lunged in and a bomb exploded throwing all of us into the floor. Kurt immediately ran to me, I was hurt but not as bad as he made it seem, Oliver had a broken arm but was okay. A hole was in the wall where the bomber once stood, as Oliver helped the other Leaders against the wall, Kurt looked out at the once glorious capital city that was now as of this moment burning to the ground.

Bombs were planted all around the city; in the markets soldiers were in firefights with Duganian rebels trying to make a difference. The city was screaming and burning trying to call out for help that was already here. Kurt, in a furious rage, stormed back in and crushed the skull of the charred corpse of the bomber under his foot.

"All troops to the Duganian border, I want their lands burnt to ash!" Two guards ran out of the door to notify the generals, Oliver stood and asked for a phone to contact his generals in case of attack on his lands. Kurt pointed the way to the nearest telephone for him, but recommended that he go see a medic first.

With the fighting increasing in the streets below, Kurt sent me to our room and sent a guard to find our kids, who were playing in the yard.

Kurt himself grabbed a weapon and went to the front of the palace where a group of guards were holding off a group of insurgents that were trying to storm the palace. The front of the palace was riddled with bullet holes, soldiers and guards lay bleeding or dead behind cover while others fire their rifles in unison mowing down insurgents in mass numbers.

"We can hold the line here my lord, but a unit down the street got taken out by a sniper, same type of skill that shot your brother, I thought you might want to check it out." Kurt clutching his rifle ran off to the downed unit to possibly find the man that took his brother from him.

Meanwhile I was in my room waiting and worrying about my husband and my kids, it wasn't long until a guard came through the door holding two small children, both were crying. When he put them down they both ran to me.

Kurt was walking through the now vacant streets of the capital, but this time nobody came. Normally people would be running through the streets, kids playing, parents laughing and have a good time, but now everyone is gone. The stillness of the world was broken once a sniper shot rang out amongst the buildings; Kurt ran into cover and waited for the second shot. The sniper fired at him, the bullet ricocheted off a wall nearby, Kurt knew that the street in front of him was to open and is a kill zone, but he ran up the street anyway. Hopping from cover to cover, just barely missing the bullet fire from the sniper. One after another the bullets came; whizzing past his head blowing his hair in the bullets shockwave. Kurt stood at the base of the sniper's tower, looking up he could see the barrel from the rifle moving from left to right looking up and down, trying desperately to find him.

 Kurt kicked in the door at the front entrance of the tower to meet whatever lay on the other side. Three insurgents stood their eyes wide not expecting what just happened, they all lunged at Kurt. He took them out simultaneously, as quietly as possible. One punch to the chest another to the head, one down, grabbing a leg and flipped onto the ground, two down. Last one, he was large, Kurt fought larger, struggled but eventually won, broke his neck. Kurt proceeded up the tower one step at a time until he reached the top, face to face with the sniper.

Looking at the sniper that had killed his brothers, his father and sister, Kurt just snapped. Throwing his gun to the side and removing a dagger from his sheath and lunged at the sniper.

The sniper blocking the lunge with his rifle said "You don't even remember me do you!" but Kurt didn't care what he said he only wanted revenge. One lunge after another, the sniper blocked every time. "It's me you fucking ass, your old friend that YOU betrayed!" Kurt finally recognized who he was fighting, a childhood friend, and a corrupted man.

"I trusted you, but all you did was hid and pretended to be a hero, while my brother led the charge!" Kurt had the sniper up against the wall.

"I got back at your brother for that…" Kurt punched him in the face, knocking some teeth out of his mouth.

"Don't you ever talk about my brother like that."

The sniper laughed, blood dripping from his mouth.

A radio sparked to life, *"Palace breached requesting sniper support!"* The sniper laughed even more while Kurt ran for the palace.

"You'll never save them in time, your whole family will burn!" Kurt could hear the sniper's laughs all the way down the road. Nothing else mattered now, Kurt stumbled and tripped running through the ruined streets of the markets, he ran all the way back to the gates of the palace.

He was too late, the trees were burning, windows smashed, and the doors were broken. Each step in the burnt grass, each crunch, was disturbing to hear. Entering through the broken door brought tears to his eyes, the floors drenched in blood, bodies strewn about from servants to soldiers. Some say everything went silent, not a man in the city yelled, nor did a woman scream, even the enemy soldiers were quiet. For the first time in years, the King cried.

"My lord? My lord?" one man stood in a hidden doorway just under the stairs. "My lord, the

Queen and kids are in the bunker, you must come!" Kurt wiped the tears from his face and followed the man to the bunker. Sneaking through the walls of the palace he could hear Duganian men looking through the rooms, checking every closet and trunk looking for something or someone. The man stood back as a door opened and he squeezed out, and then signaled for Kurt to follow. "Right down there, get to the lift and hurry." Kurt as quietly as possible stepped over ripped paintings and broken vases, trying to get to the lift. A door suddenly swung open and two men walked out.

Both wearing regular clothes, they had rifles strung over their backs, and a Duganian flag was wrapped around their right arms, they had to be rebels. They were looking for something, the man. Kurt looked back and the man was gone, he was nowhere in sight. Kurt continued making his way to the lift keeping an eye on the rebels as he did. Each step was soft and quiet, never before had Kurt moved this slowly.

The two rebels heard something move, for a second Kurt thought that they had heard him. Kurt spun around only to see the two rebels looking at a bright light that was emitting from around a doorway in the hall.

"He is here you must go now." The man from before was behind Kurt, he made no noise just appeared from nowhere. The two rebels screamed as their flesh was burned from their bones.

"We must go right now!" Kurt and the man started running for the lift as fast as they could, glancing back Kurt could see a man standing there glowing a beautiful light. Then Kurt realized the man was not touching the ground.

Kurt made it to the lift, but the man helping did not. For just a moment Kurt thought he saw the two men had wings. The humming of the lift felt weird, it was peaceful compared to the war going on above. As Kurt got farther and farther down the sounds of war got dimmer and dimmer, he was safe. But that is not what he was worried about; he wanted to see his family. The lift stopped and the doors opened, I was standing there with our two sons. He was so ecstatic, he cried and ran over to me giving me the greatest hugs. Shade and Leo held onto his legs both crying and trying to say something.

"It's okay boys, nothing will hurt you down here." They shook their heads and pointed down a dark hallway with a flickering light at the end of it. "The boys were playing down there just a little while ago, they came back crying." Kurt grabbed an electric lantern and heading down the hall both kids closely behind. One step at a time they made their way down the hall, Shade and Leo wouldn't move away from Kurt, well until he turned the corner.

Leo ran first slipping and tripping along the way, Shade followed soon after. Down in the hallway the dripping of water and Kurt's footsteps echoed, they sounded like God was walking through the halls of heaven. Kurt had entered a dark room; it smelled of mold and death. The room was glowing, a dim purple light leaking from a small black book with a ram's head on its cover.

A deep voice came from the book, "COME" it shouted loud and booming. Kurt could not resist the call, as if his will was overpowered by some unholy spell. He walked up to the book and once again the voice spoke "COME", picking up the book caused his arm to tingle and burn, he opened the book.

He collapsed to the floor as a thunderous horn sounded off nearby, his ears bled and his bones shook. Before him stood a tall monstrous creature, its eyes were as red as rubies and its body was covered in thorns. It bent down and grabbed Kurt by his head and without any effort lifted him off the ground. It pulled Kurt in close and spoke to him "YOU ARE NOT WORTHY" a sword manifested in the creature's other hand and he raised it above his head. "YOU WILL DIE" this monster was going to kill him, until a little boy shouted "Daddy!" the creature looked down. Standing before him was a young boy with fear in his eyes it was Leo, "WHY WOULD YOU STAND BEFORE WAR CHILD?"

Leo looked up, tears running down his face, and said "Because he is my daddy and he would never let anyone die so I will do the same for him!"

The creature dropped Kurt and vanished. "AN INNOCENT HAS PROTECTED YOU, BUT LET THIS BE KNOWN, THE NEXT TIME WE MEET I WILL NOT HESITATE TO KILL HIM TO…" Kurt was seriously injured and needed medical attention, I ran to find a medical kit and plugged up Kurt's ears while shade patched up his gashes and broken bones to the best we could.

Leo was sitting in the corner crying and shaking, hoping his father that he would be ok. Someone felt his hope; a young man appeared in the doorway carrying a staff, he created a peaceful aura in the room. He walked up to Kurt and removed the bandages that covered his arms and the cotton in his ears. He then began to emit a white light around Kurt; his ears stopped bleeding and his bones cracked back into place. The young man had healed him and without a single word began to walk out. I stopped him asking his name,

"My name is Raphael, but I must leave, good luck to you." He left the doorway and vanished around the corner.

CHAPTER FOUR

-BIRCHWOOD-

We were all down there for days as the battle took place above, we all began staying away from one another, especially Leo who talks to himself in the other room, but sometimes we hear a second voice coming from there, a smooth and calm voice. Every time we check no one is there and the voice goes away. One late afternoon the door to the bunker had opened and several soldiers stormed in.

Thankfully they were ours, "Thank the lord you're all okay, the palace had been bombed out, we have been digging out the ruble for the past few days." We were all crying with joy, except Leo who was just standing there with no emotion at all.

We walked out of the hole the soldiers had dug, greeted by the warm sunlight and the wrecked city that was our home. "What was the casualty count?"

Kurt asked to which the soldier responded "Around two thirds of the city's population was killed in the bombings around two thousand soldiers died in the fighting while thirty thousand Duganian rebels were killed by us and friendly fire." Kurt had to sit down that was to many people who lost their lives under his sixth year of rule. That was the least of our problems, the first was that a creature of extreme power was somewhere in the world, but that was highly classified as soon as it happened, so the "priority" was to find a fair replacement for the capital. Various towns and cities were considered but only one was perfect for the capital.

Pointing to the map Kurt just said "there" and left to pack, on the islands where he was pointing was a small city, insignificant to anyone who would pass it. But to Kurt it was the most important, no one knew why until we arrived there. As we approached the island we could see a horde of people already at the dock to see what boat was nearing. I could see people from all different lands in different and colorful clothes, all with different cultures standing side by side what a beautiful sight. After the boat docked Kurt insisted that he step off first, even though the guards advised against it.

When the people saw Kurt the all cheered "He returns! He returns!" Kurt's smile soon fell to a frown when he locked eyes with a woman holding a bunch of flowers. He walked up to her telling her of Winston's death, she dropped the flowers she was holding and collapsed to her knees. I asked Kurt what was going on and he explained to me that she was Winston's wife and technically the Queen, but that the parliament did not approve of her so she remained here instead of with Winston. "Winston always planned on returning here someday." He said to the young woman, wiping away her tears. A crewman of the boat we had arrived on walk up and told Kurt that the special package in the hull is being brought up now to which Kurt gave the man some money and asked for it to be brought down and taken to the graveyard.

    Out of the boat they brought a coffin and they walked it down to a small cemetery near a small white wooden church. Everyone walked inside. The coffin was opened to confirm who it was. A perfectly preserved Winston was inside, "How does he still look like this?" I asked, "Why is he not decayed?" Kurt just smiled and he raised his hand. A small blue flame sparked to life within his palm, "My family was one of the last that can still use magic, I never use it though, takes it out of me." That was a complete shock when he told me that, especially since his family prohibited magic from the Union.

    We closed the coffin and began to gather in the cemetery. Almost everyone had something to say about Winston; Kurt had a lot to say especially. We lowered him into the ground as the local people sung a song that Winston apparently loved. Everyone went home or back to their jobs and we went to the new headquarters on the top of a cliff just outside the town.

The soldiers were still setting up the new HQ around an old mansion. The entrance of the mansion had a sign that read *Birchwood Manor,* around it tables were set up along with radios and tents. Kurt was off talking with a man about a map of the Southern hemisphere of the Eastern continents, so while he wasn't being over protective I slipped into the manor.

The door was heavy and thick; it took all my strength to open it up. Inside it was run down and broken, furniture was broken and disheveled showing signs of some kind of fight. On the fireplace there sat about four pictures of two teen boys, of the four pictures one was a small sketch. It was a drawing of the two boys and a girl who was hugging the older boy and the young boy was holding a small decorus cub, in the bottom corner of the drawing it said Winston, Kurt, Catie, and Aishimasu. Something moved behind me, I spun around but I was to slow, it was the decorus only it was no longer a cub. The decorus was low to the ground getting ready to pounce, but before it could Kurt opened the door, "Aishimasu Yameru Kono shunkan!" the cub stood down.

"What are you doing in here?" Kurt was pissed I could see it in his eyes, "You could have been killed by any number of problems!"

"Kurt look at me I'm fine." He was still pissed at me. He glared at me while he walked over to the big black cat. "I thought decorus where red?" the cat jumped up on Kurt, his paws resting on his shoulders.

Kurt seemed as happy and the decorus, "Normally a decorus is a shade of red but this big guy is special, he was born mostly black. The only bit of red is on his head." Kurt rubbed one finger on the cat's head. "Anyway Sera how about you go check on the kids, I think they were playing near the center of town.

Walking through the center of town was different than in the capital. The town was smaller and more peaceful. The trees that give the town its name were everywhere they covered every building and every inch of the sky. The roads were made of cobble but the occasional patch of dirt would pop through. The people here were kind and answered every question I asked, they mostly gathered around the town center.

Leo was sitting by himself looking into the well, while Shade was talking to the local kids. The kids seemed amazed by the tales that Shade had to say. It was good that Shade was making new friends that were our new home for a long time. Leo continued looking into the well even though some of the kids wanted him to tell them tales, he turned at stood up from where he was sitting. Being at least three years older than most of them he was taller, he pushed through the group of smaller children and went back to the manor.

"What is wrong with Leo mother?" Shade asked he looked worried.

"I don't know," I said in response "Just leave him to himself." I was very concerned with the way Leo was acting he was usually a very proud and talkative kid. Ever since we hid in that bunker he was acting erratic and frustrated. Kurt walked into the center of town; he was met with a lot of hand shaking and free food baskets, which was good because we were out of food mostly. Kurt handed the baskets of food to the guards and gathered the boys and me. He wanted to show us something but he did not tell us. We walked to a small rowboat and we all got on. Kurt started rowing but still would not tell us where we were going, when we were out in the middle of the ocean or at least what we thought was out in the middle of nowhere Kurt lifted his hand and the blue flame returned. Shade was amazed by it and tried to imitate it, Leo just looked into the sea.

On the horizon lay a small island it was green and lush. As we approached Leo suddenly mumbled, "They are here." And then a loud and booming horn blew.

"That horn never happened before…" On the island's highest point, we could see the outline of that devilish creature from the bunker. "Damn, everyone into the water!" We all jumped into the water as the boat was blasted to pieces by a beam of some sort. We looked back at the island to find where that blast came from, a second creature this one on a horse stood on the shore. This one was decaying and covered in blisters and pus as if was sickness personified.

"OUR LORD NEEDS A VESSEL AND HE HAS CHOSEN" The two creatures raised their arms to the sky and started chanting.

"TOLLE PUERUM ET OPUS DOMINI NOSTRI VAS IPSUM ET IN IPSO SACRIFICIO RENASCI" Leo was raised from the sea and was brought before the two creatures. "HUJUS MUNDI ELEGIT DEUS IN ILLO PUERO SURREXISTI ET LUMEN QUOD IN TE" The creatures shouted and a ball of light, which exploded burning the island, then surrounded Leo. When the smoke cleared Leo was gone, but the creatures were still there.

Kurt pulled a small device from his coat pocket, just moments later we heard the battle cruiser's guns fired, the whistling of the shells became louder and louder, a bubble of some kind form around us as Kurt's nose started to bleed. The ships off the coast of Birchwood suddenly and violently bombarded the island. Whatever was left of the island was destroyed and the creatures were gone. The bubble faded away and I drug Kurt up with me and Shade to the surface. I put Kurt's body on a plank from the destroyed rowboat, he wasn't breathing.

After Kurt signaled the ships to open fire on the island I awoke floating in what was a large open space layered in a thick black fog. "Hello young Queen." The voice was echoed and loud,

"Do not panic, you are safe."

"Where am I?" I asked and the voice responded.

"Your physical body is safely aboard a ship sailing back to Birchwood, you are currently in a limbo like state so that I can talk to you."

This voice sounded so familiar but I just could not recognize it. "You're wondering who I am, but you already know me." Those words sounded so comforting and peaceful. I trusted him but I did not know who he was. "I have been sent to give you a message and a warning. Leo was taken a very powerful demon and he wished to make him his mortal form, if he does this he will be able to walk among man and rise to power. He wants to be praised and worshiped, he wants power."

These words were disturbing yet powerful if true. "How would I find him; we haven't been able to find any of the creatures"

"Those creatures are called the horsemen, there are four of them, the first being Pestilence, the next is War, the two that have yet to show are Famine and Death."

Just the thought of more of these creatures shook me to the core. I asked why they were attacking my family why did they want us.

"They have hunted your family down for generations, your grandfather, your father and mother, and even me your brother, but they could never get to you. You were too strong willed."

I could not believe my ears, Winston was speaking to me from heaven or wherever he was but I knew it was him, I could not help to stop the tears running down my face.

I wanted to see him, I needed to so I begged and pleaded but he refused. "I have no physical form for you to see, I only have those words of advice, sorry…"

Upon awaking three men immediately ran over to me. "Are you ok? We saw you and your family floating in the water when we arrived." One of the men said.

"Yes I am fine, where's Kurt and Shade?" I asked but they looked hesitant to respond.

"My lady, Kurt is fine but Shade was under too long. His brain was cut off from oxygen for at least five minutes.

Pushing the men aside I ran to my child's bedside. He was lying still on a small cot in the infirmary. I started crying fearing for the worst but then he began to breath. "Oh thank god!" I shouted hugging my son.

"He won't wake up for a long time I'm afraid." The doctor seemed very unconfident about what he was saying. "We have found old books about this condition but we have no clue on if it can be cured."

I knew what he was talking about. We know it as the sleeping sickness but the ancients called it a coma. We knew little about the ancients all we know that they were advanced in all fields of science.

"All we can do is wait and watch."

I sat by his bedside until Kurt had come to see me. Kurt eventually came but to strap Shade down to the bed he was on.

"What's going on? Why are you strapping him down?" I asked very confused.

"A recon plane spotted a Sangseungian fleet nearby we are preparing to attack." He said now strapping me and other objects down around the room.

Just seconds later the captain's voice came over the loudspeakers. "All crew to battle stations A.S.A.P. that means now people! We are heading into battle!"

Kurt gave me a kiss and ran to the bridge leaving me to look after our son. Within seconds of the alarm sounding aerial dogfights blocked out the sun. The sound of battleships firing stopped any other noise from being heard unless you had a direct head piece to the bridge. Bi-planes dropped from the sky like flies and some even kamikaze into the warring fleets. Out of the small window in my room I saw what looked like a wall coming at the ship I was on. With a huge explosion and the ship swaying sideways I realized that one of the enemy battle ships had hit us.

    A small device in the corner of the room started to blink and the rocking of ship caused it to slide across the room, but I was strapped down. Eventually, I unstrapped myself just a bit and tried to reach for the device. It was just out of my reach. I accepted that I would have to completely unstrap myself from the chair in order to grab the device.

    Waiting for just the right time I grabbed the device and fell with a very loud thud. Ignoring the pain, I inspected the device and noticed a small switch. On the top it said transmit and on the bottom it said receive; the switch sat in the middle. Upon sliding it up an incomplete voice immediately came through.

    "-forces re – to the cent – as soon – the ship

has been lost."

Panicked and afraid I grabbed my child and ran out the door. It was at this moment I realized that the ship was going down. Looking out on the horizon all I could see was death and mayhem. But at that moment all I could think of is my son; I did not care about my own safety or anyone else's. As I ran along the ship's railing I could hear gunfire within.

Near the front of the ship was an evacuation boat that can hold up to fifteen people. When I arrived, the front of the ship was up in flames with charred corpses strewn about. The smell was an overwhelming stench of burning skin and bone. The sounds of the flesh sizzling and the few people that were still alive calling for help caused me to become nauseous and gave me nightmares for the rest of my life.

"Sera! Get your head down!" Kurt shouted from the other side of the deck. At the same time a Sangseungian fighter plane flew just overhead and strafed; cutting up the center of the ship along with any human that was unfortunate enough to get caught in the attack. "Ok Sera hurry up and get over here!"

Two more Sangseungian fighters turned to make a go at a second run only for one of them to get shot down by anti-aircraft guns that were firing off every second. The remaining fighter then flew directly into the bridge of the ship killing the captain and the remaining crew. The ship then exploded and cracked in half. The explosion lit up the sky revealing the huge swarms of fighter planes circling above.

Kurt and I escaped to a nearby ship and our fleet retreated to the town of Birchwood that was just over two miles away. Once we arrived the fleet disembarked and garrisoned the town preparing for the imminent attack. The injured and the dead were placed in the Birchwood manor while anyone that could help build was building coastal defenses or digging trenches.

I was in the eastern tower of the manor looking over the town below the cliff. All the men and even the women working like ants trying to protect their home. Kurt brought Shade down to the shelter dug into the side of the cliff that was beneath the manor; he insisted I go as well but I did not want to run from the battle that approaches. It took days to prepare for the oncoming attack.

The entire beachfront was entrenched and fortified to the best of our ability as well as the jungles surrounding Birchwood. When we finished all we needed to do was wait.

CHAPTER FIVE

-BATTLE OF BIRCHWOOD-

On the twenty third of November Nineteen Twenty Eight the first day of the battle had begun. The air raid sirens sounded off and all civilians evacuated the town to the nearby bomb shelters within the cliff. Kurt and I stayed in the Headquarters that was set up in the manor; we watched and listened from the east tower as the first wave of invaders set foot on the shore.

Within the jungles all anti-air guns were pointing up and unleashing hell on the enemy air forces; one at a time they were shot from the sky. On the ground artillery and ground support opened fire on the invading force tearing them to shreds and destroying any incoming landing craft. This gave our fleet enough time and protection to deploy reinforcements and all the fighter planes we could pull from the frontlines.

Within a few minutes the sky shattered from hundreds of fighter planes shooting each other down. Each plane smashing into the ground and sea. Enemy transport planes flew overhead dropping troops into the city; one of the planes was hit with an anti-air shell and broke in two. From where I was I could see the soldiers falling from the sky with no parachute to slow them down and disappearing into the trees. Kurt begged for me to go to the bunkers but once again I refused, "Just as you stand by your soldiers, I shall stand by you." I said.

The day moved slow as the battle grew near. The ground beneath my feet shook with every detonation and with every gunshot my heart sank further and further. I could not eat that night; at least not while knowing that the city below me was drenched in the blood of soldiers and even more were dying every second of the day.

By eight in the morning the entire

surrounding area was burning from the fighting. Birchwood was barely there. Buildings fell where they stood, crushing anyone inside. Near the center of town, a bomber had crashed and the pilot was still alive; missing one of his legs he crawled to the sidewalk only to be picked off by a sniper.

Later that day I was sitting in my room waiting for Kurt when a bullet came through the window. Before I knew it I couldn't breathe. The bullet had pierced my throat and I was bleeding out. Kurt ran in when he heard the gunshot and found me on the floor. He tried to cover my wound but it would not have helped. I was dying in his arms and there was nothing anyone could do.

In my last moments of life, I placed my hand on his heart and smiled.

"No please don't leave, please not you to..."

CHAPTER SIX

-HUNTED-

His world became colder than anything else. Carrying my body down to the bunker below; his heart no longer felt. He no longer cared for the world around him; he just wanted this war to end and that meant all options are on the table. Kurt laid me on a cot in the back rooms and covered me with a blanket, after that he called General Dāo, the commander of this battle, to the planning room.

Kurt gave him all the details about the sniper that has been following him and his family. "His name is Kirā-Jū, he is an extremely skilled sniper from the Northern Union near Sangseungia. He was with the first settlers that came here to Birchwood. He was a young boy back then, and so was I." General Dāo was shocked, not one person knew Birchwood existed and even less knew it was founded by the two sons of King Bàojūn Black. After a moment of confusion in made sense to the general. Kurt gave General Dāo a description of Kirā-Jū; the general handed the description to several couriers who then dispersed it to the front lines.

- Average sized male, black short hair, scar down his left eye, around twenty years of age-

The courier's race to the fronts to find anyone who has seen the sniper, they will arrive on the second day of the Battle of Birchwood.

The beachhead was taking heavy hits but still holding. One of the couriers was running through the trenches that were hastily dug in the sand tripping has she ran to find the commanding officer. All around her were dead bodies and soldiers fighting while overhead planes fought in vicious aerial dogfights. She seemed hesitant to bring her head up to look around and she had every right to do so. Every time she would look up bullets would still be flying over her head.

She ran over the bodies of men who died peaking over the trench wall. Looking through the trenches for anyone who can help her find the commanding officer she eventually found a wounded soldier being helped by a frontline medic.

"Can you point me to your commanding officer, I have very important information for him." She said crouching down next to them.

The medic pulled a bandage tight around a soldier's arm causing the soldier to scream. "He should be on the other side of the beach, more towards the back."

"What happened here?" She asked while holding back some vomit from seeing, running and now crouching in so much blood.

"A sniper ambushed us from behind; son of a bitch cut a path right through us." He lifted the soldier over his shoulder and started carrying him away and the courier, now knowing that the sniper came through here ran even faster than before.

The slush of the wet and blood soaked sand was sickening. Each step was another chance of stepping in human remains or tripping on a rifle.

The courier eventually made it to the commanding officer; except the officer was shot through the head, on him was a small letter from one of the other fronts.

"We require reinforcements on the Northern Jungle Front, the Duganians have arrived and have landed troops on the farthest north point of the island. Heavy tanks and anti-personnel vehicles being deployed. We have also sent word to the king that the sniper he is looking for is held up in a church in the center of town."

The courier ran back to the king and arrived at dusk; she relayed the information to him, he grabbed a small pistol and set out on his own.

Kurt made his way to the center of the town and he found the church. He opened the door as slow as he possibly could and walked inside. The church was empty, there was absolutely no living being inside the building. Under the large mural of the gods lay a sleeping man, Kirā-Jū.

Kurt walked up to slowly and cautiously move his gun away. Kurt pulled out his pistol and pointed it at Kirā-Jū. He woke up to a gun barrel pointed in his face and was then immediately knocked out.

CHAPTER SEVEN

-IMPRISONED-

Kirā-Jū woke up sitting in a chair, arms strapped down, and in a lot of pain. Kurt stood by a small table just a few feet away. He was facing away from Kirā-Jū sorting through some tools.

"So Kirā-Jū, welcome to my little horror show!" The surrounding room was dark and it smelt terrible; like the inside of a rotting corpse. "You have really pissed me off these past years so now I'm going to deal with you." Kurt walked over to another table and picked up a scissor and walked over to Kirā-Jū. "Do you know how to stop a sniper from sniping…? Off with their trigger finger!"

Kurt grabbed Kirā-Jū's pointer finger on his

left hand and with a crunch he cut it off. Kirā-Jū screamed in pain but Kurt just tied his mouth with a cloth.

Kurt held up the finger "One down ten to go" he held down Kirā-Jū's left hand and cut them off one by one. Each finger snapped and crunched as it was cut through the bone.

Kirā-Jū begged to be killed but Kurt did not care, he moved over to the table and picked up a long knife and stabbed through Kirā-Jū's right hand. He screamed in pain; for mercy. Kurt, even more furious from his pleads for forgiveness and mercy, covered his hands in a magical blue flame and grabbed Kirā-Jū's head engulfing it in flames.

The screams could be heard throughout the empty building, no one heard his screams and no one came to help, everyone had fled to the bunkers. The flames burnt his eyelids shut and his ears to his head.

Kurt looked at the horror that he created and smiled a crooked smile. The fires in his hands extinguished and Kurt turned to walk out of the room each step was torture to Kirā-Jū, the echo from each step was murder to Kirā-Jū's burning ears. Standing in the frame of door Kurt began to laugh louder and louder.

"I hope you burn in Hell!" Kirā-Jū screamed at Kurt over and over. Yelling and struggling to move his body.

"I'll see you there." Kurt slammed the door and from behind it, within the dark corners of the room came a shadow. It whispered to him in a soft female voice.

"Hello there Kirā-Jū I've been watching you for such a long time now." This shadow started to form into a woman standing nude before him. *"I have a proposition for you… I can give you extraordinary power you just have to give me something in return…"* Kirā-Jū pondered for a moment not knowing if to trust only what he hears and cannot see.

"I'm listening" He said very cautiously and the shadow knew it. "What is your name first of all since you seem to already know mine." His voice was broken and hoarse from screaming in pain.

"You may call me Babylon the Great, mortal."

Her voice remained calm which was unnerving. *"So what do you say Kirā-Jū do you agree?"*

"I'll agree to anything as long as Kurtis Theodore Black dies tonight!" Babylon smiled and transformed back into a shadow. It began to engulf Kirā-Jū.

"You'll get your wish as I will get mine, Kurtis will die but so will thy!" The shadow flew into Kirā-Jū's mouth and for a moment he sat still. Then a twitch. Eventually his body began to thrash about and become something new.

Kirā-Jū began to settle but when he looked up he was no longer himself. Where Kirā-Jū once sat now sat Babylon. With one pull the straps holding her down broke of and she was free. She pushed the door out of its hinges and calmly strutted down the hall to find her objective.

Each step she made was a forceful one. As she walked the ground shook; she shouted in strange unknown words. Kurt was standing on the spot where I died, looking out the window at the carnage being brought down on this lonely island.

"Kurtis Theodore Black, I have come for your

head." Kurt turned around just in time to dodge a swinging blade. Kurt quickly grabbed a rifle from the table nearby but Babylon's sword cut right through it. Kurt ran through the halls of the manor trying to find an open room to get his bearings and they eventually made it to the roof of the manor. Kurt clasped his hands together and pulled them apart slowly. Each finger of his started to spark and electricity began to jump between them. He pulled back and struck forward at Babylon who nimbly moved out of the way of the electric whip.

"Why are you here? Who are you?" Kurt asked in between evading sword swipes and kicks. The ground continued to shake and move beneath the island. Soon Babylon got sick of this game and decided the only way to kill Kurt was by using brute force not with fancy sword skills. She went to the edge of the roof and jumped. As she fell the ground opened and out came a hideous beast. The Beast ate her as she fell and roared; its bottom jaw split and six small tongues came out, each with mouths as well. Upon its head were ten horns and its hide was rough and red. Kurt was face to face with The Beast and was about to be eaten as well when three explosions detonated near the monsters left set of eyes. To Kurt's shock they were Duganian and Union planes flying side by side to destroy this hell spawn.

The Beast turned to the newly unified armies and let out another fearsome roar. It began to make its way out towards the armada of Sangseungian, Duganian, and Union ships that fired everything they got at it. Planes flew it and around the shell fire shooting at every part of the monster. Every soldier scattered when it moved then found a new position and opened fire on The Beast. It raised its head and screamed, Kurt had gone back inside to try and get to the underground bunker. The Monster then placed its jaw up against the side of the manor and each of the tongues had started to slither out farther and farther looking for Kurt. They made weird noises every now and then almost as if they were communicating with each other. Kurt moved as quietly as possible.

The each mouth made a separate noise each causing a different feeling. One made a quiet clicking noise that would vary in speed making Kurt want to run while another made a smooth humming noise causing him to become sleepy. Kurt was braced up against the wall just beside a doorway when one slithered up beside him. Its skin was transparent Kurt could see every pulsing vein underneath. It stopped near him and underneath its skin Kurt could see a large gelatinous eye; and it looked right at him. The tongue turned to strike Kurt, Kurt ducked out of the way and began running down the long manor hall. The tongues twisted and turned but couldn't extend to keep up with Kurt.

One tongue was blocking the exit and lunged at Kurt. He pulled out a small dagger and slid on his knees beneath the tongue driving the blade straight through the tongue splitting it in half. It screamed and The Beast roared; the tongues left and The Beast now clawed at the manor trying to rip it off the mountain side. Kurt ran out of the door leading to the mountain path towards the town. The armies continued their assault but The Beast was focused on Kurt.

The Beast tried to snap at Kurt as he ran down the mountainside. Kurt tripped on every other stone as this monster came crashing down on the path at the same time as artillery shells came down from the distant fleet. The guns rang out in the far horizon and not to long after The Beast was hit with about thirty shells. A few managed to penetrate its thick hide and cause it to bleed although the skin would heal over very quickly almost making it immortal, almost. Kurt had noticed that the wound stayed open long enough for a bomber to get a bomb in. Kurt ran down the mountain path and eventually made it into Birchwood.

    Kurt made it through most of the town without being seen by The Beast. The town was ripped to shreds, buildings were burnt and bodies of Union and Duganian soldiers were scattered about beaten and bloodied from battle. A plane flew down close to the ground; it was Union and it spotted him. Kurt held out in a building nearby waiting for troops to find him, so Kurt could tell them his plan.

    Upon waking the next day Kurt heard movement from outside. It was Duganian troops on a march, they seemed to be looking for someone. One spotted Kurt and they all turned in one quick movement and began to walk over.

    "Are you the King of the Union" he said in very poor Unionese.

Kurt was hesitant to reply "Um. Yes." the Duganian walked over and handed him a report from General Nokota, the main general for the Birchwood defense. It read…

This letter is only for the eyes of The King of The Union Kurtis Theodore Black if he still lives.

Sir, all troops have moved back to the shore line. Every hour or so that monster starts digging through the rubble to find something. We suspect it's trying to get at the civilians within the mountain. We are currently working with Dugania and Sangseungia to defeat this demonic monstrosity and a few have even been willing enough to join our cause and even heal any wounded troops with magic.

- General Nokota

CHAPTER EIGHT

-THE BEAST-

Kurt looked up at the nearby Duganian soldiers who were now just leaning against a nearby wall. One started poking the ground with his gun.

"So, do you know where General Nokota is?" none of the Duganians had a clue about what Kurt said. They all just stood there and looked with blank expressions. Kurt just started walking away. Kurt could hear the monster in the distance... moving... searching. The town was quiet and dead, not even a bird cried in the trees, no wind blew through the streets, skeletons lined every corner. Strange.

Soon Kurt arrived at the shore line and met with General Nokota.

"My lord, it's great to see that you live." General Nokota bowed to Kurt in which Kurt bowed back slightly lower.

"General Nokota, I know how to take that thing down." General Nokota looked intrigued and urged Kurt to follow him into the nearby tent. Within the tent sat two generals and three admirals, each from their respective Empires. They all stood as Kurt entered the tent.

"Your majesty, we have called a permanent truce at least between the armies in this area. As you can see all of us agree with the danger that faces us." General Nokota said while he sat down at the far end of the table.

"I'm afraid that General Nokota and in fact all of you do not know the full story." The group of generals were intrigued and most definitely confused. "The world, gentlemen, is coming to an end. At Least the way we see the world that is."

"You're saying the world is ending… do you have any proof?" The Sangseungian admiral asked standing up from the table. Kurt walked over to a little flap in the side of the tent that acted as a window, Kurt then pointed to the large monster digging into the mountain.

"There's your proof!" Kurt said emphasizing on his words. "That thing is from hell sent to kill all the people on this island, all the people that know." Kurt looked at all the men around the table. All of whom look terrified.

The tent went silent. No one stood. No one spoke. Kurt walked around the table and sat keeping the stern look on his face. The sound of fighting grew as a soldier ran into the tent with a message.

"There is a fight starting on the airfield, two Duganian soldiers began to taunt some of the Union guys. Others joined in the fight and it's not going so well for anybody."

Kurt and some of the nearby soldiers left the meeting and went to the makeshift airfield. Three Union airmen were in a scuffle with two Duganian soldiers; multiple soldiers, airmen, and seamen had encircled them and were all betting on who would win. Kurt brought his gun out of its holster and fired it into the air. One Duganian began to curse out who ever fired but quickly stopped upon seeing who it was.

"Who the hell started this fight!" Kurt shouted gun still smoking. "Tell me right now or all of you will be standing on the bad end of a firing squad!" None of the soldiers moved they all stared unknowing of what to do.

Kurt ordered one of the soldiers to grab a Union airman and hold him at gunpoint while the other soldier grabbed a Duganian soldier and did the same. The surrounding crowd was shocked and silent awaiting the consequences. The Unionite and the Duganian both pleaded for mercy and it did not take long until the other generals showed up.

"What is this, release my man at once!" General Alttanin demanded and began to walk towards the Duganian captive.

"If you take one more step General I will take the shot myself, now please take a few steps back." Kurt raised his gun and aimed at the soldier's head. Alttanin stopped and looked at Kurt with a penetrating stare; Kurt did not back down. The air between was so dense you could feel the tension. Alttanin took out his sidearm and aimed it at the union soldier.

"You shoot my man and I shoot yours." No one moved.

Kurt, still aiming at the Duganian soldier, slowly pulled out his blade and in one quick movement Kurt threw it through the Duganian soldier's head. Alttanin turned to shoot the Union soldier only to find a gun pointed directly at his face. All soldiers were armed and aiming at one another. The peace between the two armies was about to shatter and suck the island back into chaos when everyone began to lower their weapons. To the outside looking in it would look like everyone just came to their senses but to them it was much different.

A voice spoke to them all, it was soft and calming. It explained to them that the world is more important than any conflict, and that they need to save as many people possible for the oncoming calamity. All minds returned to the pressing issue. The mission was handed out to all pilots, Tank squads, and artillery men. The Goal: damage the beast's skin and create a hole large enough for a missile to detonate with in.

The attack commenced immediately. Everyone got in positions and opened fire on the massive beast that stood to destroy the world. Artillery flew across the sky and crashed all along its back while the tanks launched everything they got at its ribs and legs. The monster roared in pain and began to tear through the ground forces.

Out from the sunlight dove an armada of planes unleashing everything they had at the beast. Island was surrounded by large dreadnoughts from all nations that soon launched everything they got at the open wound that had been carved into the monster's ribs.

Tons of explosive shells rained down from the sky, all of which impacted the creature's exposed side. It fell from the blast sending a shock wave of air across the entire island. The blast also knocked off a chunk of the mountain covering the bunker. The civilians were now out in the open.

The Beast began to rise. Weak yet alive. Planes began to circle back around when the sun was blocked out. A zeppelin larger than any other before large enough to carry every civilian out of the war zone.

It landed on the nearest stretch of open field it could find and radioed out for anyone to start evacuating civilians to the craft. All radios had picked up the signal and the mission went from an attack to an evacuation. All armies began protecting the civilians long enough to get them to the zeppelin. Planes dove full speed into the beast while ground troops unleashed a barrage of gun and artillery fire at its legs. This was our last hope in stopping this Devil.

The creature raised up and spewed flames scorching the mountain side and spreading the fire throughout the island. Men, women and children burned alive in the ongoing inferno. Most had made their way back to the zeppelin in time for takeoff. The engines began to start and the aircraft began to rise. They had made it. They had survived this hell. Or at least that is what they thought in that moment. One of the engines had caught fire and was about to blow.

At maximum height it blew causing the ship to begin to lean to the side of the island. In a quick moment the pilot told all the survivors to make peace with their gods and loved ones, the ship was going to crash back into the monster.

The view was devastating to those on the ground but to those inside it was worse. Mothers held to their children. Most men were silent. The flames began to engulf the hull and soon it began to make its way inside. The sky turned red with fire as it streaked across the horizon. The impact was bright and silent, then the sound hit. A thunderous boom then silence once more.

No Monster.

No Fighting.

No Cheering.

Just Silence.

Then came the sound.

The sound of an entire world losing hope.

CHAPTER NINE
-AFTERMATH-

With the monster dead, they were left to wonder; what now. If it took all that to kill that beast how could they be ready for what might come next. Kurt wasn't concerned about that. He just sat by his son's bedside and waited for him to awake all the while searching for the way to tell Shade what had happened to me, to Leo, to everyone.

No one spoke that much for the next few days. They just followed orders and began to clean up the mess. Taking count of the men each army lost. How much damage was caused? Reinforcements arrived not long after to help clean up, bury the bodies, and reinforce the island.

Soldiers came in confused at the peace on the island. To them the Union of Democratic Republics had surrendered to Dugania. It was good to let them think that, kept people from knowing. The new soldiers were not prepared for what they saw on the island. Every living soldier and general looked just as dead as the soldiers that had died, just as blank.

A small scout party had been deployed out near the zeppelin crash site to look for survivors. They went expecting nothing but death and destruction but came back with three surviving members. One a mother holding the partially charred remains of a bear toy, the others two teen boys too terrified to speak. All three were sent to the infirmary for checkup and some rest. The mother refused to eat or drink and died weeks later.

The generals tried to come up with a plan on how to survive the destruction of the world but none could compensate the other's idea. They just argued over and over. Kurt stayed by Shade's side and denied any invite. It took months but the island was finally fortified and the teen boys began to talk. They explained that the pilot had gone mad, something we would debunk a decade later.

Kurt eventually came around and began sitting at the meetings though he did not speak. He took notes. Every demand made by one leader was countered by another demand by another leader. It wasn't until Oliver came in from the Sui'nian Federation to join the talks.

"We all thought you were dead! How could

you just vanish without letting your allies know?" Oliver was furious.

"This is larger than any war Oliver…" Kurt did not finish his sentence before Oliver cut him off.

"How can anything be bigger than losing everything you've worked for everything you've care about?" Kurt struck Oliver across his face. Oliver collapsed still holding a nearby table but barely able to stand.

"I already have! Can't you see that?" Kurt took a deep breath and calmed down slightly. "Sera is dead. Leo was taken. Shade won't wake." Oliver regretted everything he just said. But then a look of curiosity arrived on his face.

"You said Leo was taken. Taken by whom?" Kurt looked up at Oliver with disbelief of what he was about to say.

"Demons"

Oliver went white and looked dead for a bit. He turned to Kurt and told him very quietly "I need to see Shade. Right. Now" Kurt walked over to the side of the tent they were in and lifted a curtain to a second room. Shade was gone.

The tent wall was burnt from the inside out

and charred footsteps lead out into the jungle. Oliver ran after them and Kurt followed. Trees had black and burnt hand marks where he stumbled, the path was clear; he was heading to the manor. The jungle smelled of decay and fire.

They heard a yell in the distance followed by a large burst of air and an explosion. The manor was no more and standing in the ruble was an older Shade. He had been changed somehow. As if the coma was a cocoon. His hair had turned white and his eyes became blue, his clothes were burnt on the tips and shredded. Upon seeing him Oliver kneeled and lowered his head.

"Master you have been reborn." Oliver did not move but Kurt didn't care. He walked up to Shade and hugged him. Shade hugged back and began to cry.

"It's good to see you dad."

Oliver stood and asked Kurt to step back from Shade. Kurt refused and Shade asked his father to sit down. Kurt sat on a remaining chair and Shade began to explain what had happened.

Shade explained that when he fell unconscious a voice began to speak to him. The voice was smooth and calm; it had explained to Shade what was happening to him. Shade had been chosen to be humanity's beacon of hope. That he and only he could bring peace and stability to the world. Shade continued and explained that every few thousand years there is a cycle to keep humanity in line and stop them from destroying the order of everything. This has been called many things, Ragnarok, Kali Yuga, al-Qiyamah, and Armageddon just to name a few that he states.

Kurt nods and Shade is surprised by his quick acceptance of the situation. "How are you not shocked by this news father?" Shade asks not expecting to hear that Kurt was attacked by a demon that had already explained half the things that are going on.

Oliver continues the conversation, hoping to return to the camp before someone notices they're gone. Although I'm sure the explosion gave that away. "Shade is one of two "prophets" that will arrive on this cycle; I assume the other will be Leo. But twin prophets rarely ever happen."

"What do you mean Leo will be the other?" Shade asked not knowing that Leo had been taken just after he had fallen unconscious. This news came as a shock to Shade but Oliver continued anyway, to Kurt's unnerve.

"Leo was taken by The Horsemen, most

likely to be converted to become the second Prophet. The second Prophet's goal is to destroy civilization and leave humanity to rot in its own destruction. He has to be stopped but it unknown when he will reappear."

Shade became dizzy and had to sit down Kurt helped him down onto the ground as Oliver continued talking.

"The only way to stop him is to kill him an-" Kurt punched Oliver knocking him to the ground.

"Can't you see Shade is uncomfortable with what you're saying, are you that thick-witted." Kurt helped up Shade and began walking him back to camp. Oliver sat on the ground for a bit wondering what he did wrong then got up and followed them back.

Arriving back at camp they discover that the Sangseungian's have begun attacking the armies that currently inhabit the island. They did not believe the fact the world was ending and decided to win this war themselves. Just after Kurt and Oliver left word arrived that Sangseungia had bombed and annexed Sui'nia and swept into northern U.D.R territory. Duganian Troops are holding the line in the frozen north.

Shade noticed a group of Union soldiers

about to be executed by Sangseungian's and began to run towards them. Arriving just in time Shade was able to give off enough heat to melt the bullets before they hit and was not injured in any way.

The Sangseungians dropped their weapons and surrendered on the spot. Shade looked at his hands amazed at what he could do. More Sangseungians arrived and prepared to shoot Shade. Kurt pulled out his sidearm and began to fire at the reinforcements.

Hitting several in the head before getting behind cover. Shade began sending fire in multiple directions burning and melting enemy soldiers and their weapons.

A tank came rolling through a nearby building and began firing at Shade who just shrugged off the bullets. The tank fired a round at him and he caught it then exploded. The smoke cleared and Shade was standing in the blast. He began to walk forward and his hand began to glow a cherry red.

He laid his hand on the front of the tank and it melted through. Shade grabbed the engine and ignited the fuel causing the tank to erupt in flame. As the crew ran out Kurt mowed them down with waves of bullets from his gun.

The sight before them was one of destruction as Shade unleashed a hell storm of fire. The heat from the flames was so intense it melted vehicles to the ground and seared men to steel.

The Sangseungian Army began to retreat to boats that were deployed from the Navy that was fighting just off shore. Just as they were about to get on the boats exploded and through the fires Shade stood there. Turning the water to steam around him.

"Surrender this instant and no one else will be injured I can assure you. But if you do not surrender I will have to take matters into my own hands and I will destroy your entire naval fleet." Shade's eyes began to glow a sky like blue as did the fires that he conjured around him. One by one each soldier raised their rifle and aimed it at Shade. "Very well…"

Shade turned his back to the soldiers on the beach and with a snap of his fingers every ship in the Sangseungian fleet erupted in flames. The screams of the people on board could be heard from shore. The capital ship exploded and sent a shock wave large enough to knock a few soldiers of their feet.

Union planes flew over the ships still

remaining afloat and carpet bombed their decks and hulls until they all sank into the depths of the sea. Duganian troops cleared the north side of the island while Union troops rounded up the stragglers on the southern side.

The Battle of Birchwood had come to an end for a second time.

Kurt walked over to Shade after the troops had been taken away. Shade turned and gave his father a great hug, Kurt began to cry. "I thought I lost you." Kurt said through his shaky voice.

"I thought I lost you too." Shade held Kurt close with tears streaming down his face.

Just seconds later the horn blew for all aboard and they rushed to get on the ship. Shade went to the dining area after using all that energy to "ignite" as he called it he needed to replenish it all. Kurt went to his quarters and unpacked. He always hated boats ever since he was taken from his mother by one. He never spoke about it.

The cramped room was the largest one they had. A small cot was in the corner with a metal desk in the corner. Kurt had placed a picture of me holding the two boys when they were babies on it. He smiled somethings that he rarely ever does. The swaying of the boat caused some of the crew to become sick and flee to the ship deck and vomit off the side.

An officer knocked on Kurt's door and allowed himself in.

"Sir, the other leaders are ready for you." The officer seemed nervous. Kurt walked passed him and gave him a pat on the shoulder.

The Leader of the Duganian Resistance and King Oliver were waiting in the lower storage of the ship to discuss how to distribute land for the three countries.

Oliver wanted all of Sangseungia, General Alttanin wanted The Duganian Empire to be restored to its formal glory, while Kurt wanted all Empires to dismantle and join together in one large Union. They argued for hours and by the end of it General Alttanin and Kurt had agreed that the two Empires will unite under one flag while Oliver stays sovereign and gets Sanqseungia.

The name of the country was decided by General Alttanin, he chose the name The Democratic Union of Dugania. It is the largest country the world has ever seen.

By the time they came to an agreement the sun had set and most of the ship had gone to sleep.

Kurt walked through the silent ship. It seemed too peaceful for being in the middle of a world war.

Shade's room was quiet and understandably so after what he did that day. Kurt opened his door to find Shade sitting on his bed holding the picture of me that was on Kurt's desk.

"I can't believe mother is gone. I've been wondering how she died but I know that I wouldn't like it." Shade began to tear up. Kurt sat down beside him.

"She never left your side son; I want you to know that. She loved you probably more than anything else on this planet." Kurt put his hand on Shade's back and told him to go back to his room and get some sleep. Kurt fell asleep not long after.

The next morning was misty and the fog was dense. The ship became slow to navigate the sea between Birchwood and Altrazi. The Sea was known as Ikiryō no umi, "Sea of Wraith". Countless ships have gone down in that area. Some say it was a sea monster that brought down the ships but it was something more natural. The waves deep in the sea got large enough to tip over the largest of any navy.

The crew is all on deck and keeping an eye out for any large waves. Below deck Kurt was writing up the document that would join The Union of Democratic republics and The Duganian Empire together. The captain was finding a quicker route to Altrazi while avoiding any danger zones. Shade spent most of his time below deck with the captain's daughter not that the captain knew of it.

The days became long and rough. Several sailors on the ship became terribly sick and died. The rest of the invasion fleet was doing just as bad. Multiple men had fallen ill and many more had begun to die. They would have to land on the shores of The Union overwhelmed with Duganians with an army low on manpower. But the time has come, shore was in sight.

CHAPTER TEN
-OPERATION FALSE PROPHET-

The morning was calm and quite. The men were getting ready, grabbing their guns and fixing their bayonets. The planes began to start up their engines and the boats were being prepared to be lowered into the sea. Soon the shore lit up to reveal a series of large artillery guns lining the coast all of which were surrounded by thousands of Duganian troops.

The horn blew giving the signal to begin deployment. Soldiers began running to the boats and dropped to the sea. The guns onshore fired sending shells into the sea around the ships and the boats. One shell hit a boat of ten soldiers directly sending the bodies and limbs of the men flying through the air leaving the remains of the wooden boat floating in the water. By this time the planes began to fly. Dropping bombs and even grenades on the enemy soldiers on land. The Duganians became confused at the three flags flying over the invading army, one Duganian, one Union, and one Sui'nian.

They had all thought to be dead but there they are and they're heading right for the shore. A once peaceful shore line filled with families was now a living hell covered in corpses washing up from the sinking boats. The sky became filled with smoke and fire as fighter planes clashed with one another some being shot down from the anti-air guns mounted along the city streets. The ocean became red with blood and still the men kept fighting getting closer and closer to the entrenched shore forces.

The ships deploying troops began to fire their guns ripping into the shore. Shrapnel flew out of the explosions some large enough to tear men in half. The boats finally landed on the shore only to be met with machine gun fire which mowed down troops before they could even get to the dry sand.

Artillery opened fire once more this time aimed more at the larger ships. One shell hit a battle ship right in the center shredding through the hull and splitting the ship in half. The front half of the ship had started tilting up sending any remaining people on the front of the ship sliding down the deck into the burning oil lying on the water.

The other landing points were having the

same luck. The entire western coast of Duganian controlled U.D.R was heavily fortified and some of the other landing points were completely lost.

It took more than five hours but enough troops landed on shore in order to overrun the Duganian fortifications and claimed the shore. The troops took to the trenches and began to retake the original capital of The Union, Altrazi. Bullets flew across no man's land striking soldiers in the head and wounding others. The city became a deadly warzone like no other before. Every building and every street had fighting. Kurt and Shade landed on shore to direct the troops towards the manor. Fighting continued through the day and even into the night. Rebelling Duganians wore white bands on their sleeves so soldiers can see who they were fighting.

Some rebels even took off their bands to get behind the enemy lines and kill them from within their trench. This made the fighting very fast and bloody with hundreds of soldiers on both sides dying every thirty seconds. Not one could take a step without stepping in a puddle of blood or tripping over a dead soldier. The smell was strong, burning bodies filled the air. Shade couldn't stand the smell and began to vomit; Kurt has become use to it.

Kurt gave the signal and all the allied soldiers bunkered down where they stood and several men wearing heavy armor began walking out of the trenches. One took a bullet to the head and it ricocheted off. The soldiers had large cylinders on their backs and were holding long tubes. The Duganians had never seen anything like this they laughed at the stupidity that they thought they saw. *"One man with a tube what could that do?"* That's what it looked like until one turned the end of the tube and huge wafts of flames lunged from the front igniting everything that it made contact with.

This was the legendary Union Ke Ahi, Union fire. The fire stuck to men and was not able to be put out. It would ignite even on water and ice. Nothing could work to stop it not even the strongest Duganian Mage. The Union soldiers who use this are protected by the thick armor but the cylinders were known to explode and that is exactly what Kurt had planned and the users knew this. Their goal is to do as much damage as they can; even if that means to self-destruct. Several of the men did just that. Large amounts of liquid flames flew in all directions melting through stone and wood.

The whistle blew and all the soldiers charged at the Duganian forces. Plunging their bayonets deep into the hearts of the enemy. In just a few minutes the manor was within sight. The Duganians held the manor and flew their flag high. The allied army charged the manor and was being gunned down; they held the walls and needed to fall.

This was the moment that changed the outcome of the entire war for a new weapon was unveiled. The grenade launcher, they brought it up to the front and fired a small grenade up into a small window. The grenade blew and destroyed the section of the wall allowing enough the soldiers through to start attacking from behind. The soldiers fought their way through the wall corridors and rooms trying to clear and capture the outer defenses. Other soldiers stormed the court yard and began to fight hand to hand with Duganians who held the barracks.

Kurt and Shade advanced to the manor and pushed through the fighting. Kurt's home and the center of the Union had been defaced. The shields that once lined the walls of the main hall had been removed and the few still in the hall were being used to block up the windows. The mural of the gods had been shot at, even painted over in some places. They traversed the broken and decayed halls looking for anything they could salvage as a symbol of the past. The battle outside raged louder and louder as it drew closer. A large concussive blast blew open the doors to the manor and the Union had begun to retake the manor. Even though there is really nothing to retake.

Soon the flag of a unified land flew over the manor. The flag of The New Union. A white flag, five red stars to symbolize the states, one blue circle to symbolize unity, and in the middle a white crescent moon a symbol of peace its flame always burning.

The world began to see hope on the horizon. That soon the entire world could unify like two waring nations who have forgiven all past sins. The Duganian Empire would only last two more years, due to economic distress and the combined might of three armies they could have never lasted much longer. At the same time, Shade took his place on the throne, the monarchy restored, and Kurt had vanished; his son now a man and his wife long dead. No one needed his guidance any longer.

But that is why you're here is it not? You have sat and patiently listened only to hear the beginning when you want to hear the end…

Is that right, Crimson?

Epilogue
-Three Years-

1929年11月28日

It's been one year since the war ended and The Union of Democratic Republics merged with The Duganian Empire. One year of my rule. I have sent scouts out to look for my Father; they have come back with nothing of significance.

Workers have been digging through the remains of the Birchwood manor searching for any remains or objects of interest. A book was found in the basement it was closed, locked in fact. I remember these books and I had it safely disposed of. I hope that my father isn't out looking for more of these books, we don't want more horsemen.

Yesterday soldiers had given searching for my mother in the Birchwood manor. The bunker underneath had completely collapsed and no body was found. Her official and public funeral was yesterday as well. I had to watch from my balcony. They brought a coffin up the street it was surrounded by soldiers and the Duganian flag was draped over it.

The world is changing but if it's for the better or for the worse that is something no one knows.

1930年6月2日

Cities in the Greater Union have begun extensive reconstruction. It's taken over a year to begin repairs but I'm glad it's finally going to start. So many cities and towns were ripped apart by the horrors of war, so many families lost.

The public reception for me is mixed. The Unioners love me as does the Sui'nians who has accepted the ultimatum and have join The Greater Union. The Duganians on the other hand care little for me and the new government. To fix this I have sent more soldiers to the region to show power, protection, and prosperity. That was Oliver's idea.

In better news I met someone. She is beautiful. Her hair sways in the wind when she walks and is as black as the darkest night. Her eyes are amazing, they sparkle like the night sky and glow with joy no matter how sad things get. I'm going to introduce myself but I don't know if she would want to date a prince.

    Her name is Akiko.

1930年6月4日

    She said yes. She is coming to the castle in the mountains. I am so excited.

1930年8月15日

    It's been almost three years since my father left and we still have no sign of him.

    I wish he was here to see me, getting married, winning wars, expanding across the globe. I'm sure where ever he is he will see the Great Union Army marching across the world.

1931年9月21日

Well today is my birthday. Only Akiko seems to care. I am technically nineteen so according to the laws my father set up I can "officially" be king. Akiko seems joyful today.

1931年9月22日

We are moving back to Birchwood today, they finally rebuilt the manor and the town. Although I wouldn't know if anyone would want to return to the site of a massacre.

1931年9月24日

A letter arrived for me today telling me that the third horsemen book was stolen before it could be disposed of. This may have put a nail in my coffin.

1931年9月27日

It finally happened, someone spotted my father in Barbaria. Why is he all the way up there? What or who is he looking for?

1931年10月1日

    A volcano just erupted in central Dugania and it sent an ash cloud across The Greater Union. It killed a lot of our crops and the blast sent flaming rock throughout the nation several nearby cities suffered damage, cities farther out got hit by earthquakes and aftershocks. The earthquakes sent out waves large enough to engulf entire cities on the southern coast of Barbaria.

Made in the USA
Middletown, DE
09 April 2017